Maria's Ghost

By

T S LIGHT

Table of Contents

ACKNOWLEDGEMENTS

I would like to express my heartfelt gratitude to my family for their unwavering belief in me. A special thank you to my son, Shawn, for always reminding me that I'm not a total screw-up. Your support has meant the world to me.

DEDICATION

To Shawn, Wanda, Edgar, Evan, Marilyn, and Kala.

My beautiful, perfect, loving, dysfunctional family, I love you.

No reason to change.

You're perfect.

ABOUT THE AUTHOR

My name is **Dianna Schlies**, My last name is often difficult for people to pronounce, so I use the pen name T S LIGHT, which is simple, easy to remember, and more accessible for readers. I'm a 70-year-old widow. Growing up, terms like ADHD, ADD, and dyslexia hadn't even been coined yet, and I was told I would never be a successful writer. For many years, I believed those words. However, it was my son who encouraged me to pursue my dream and get my work published, and I'm forever grateful for his support.

Born in Texas and raised in Silver City, NM, I've spent a lifetime proving that it's never too late to follow your passion. Today, I stand proudly as a testament to perseverance and the power of never giving up on your dreams.

EPILOGUE

What do you think of when you hear the word ghost?

Footsteps in an empty room?

Voices when no one is around?

What about beautiful, talented, funny, or even scared of you?

No, then allow me to introduce you to Maria Dalgodo.

CHAPTER 1

Let's go back to how this all began. Sarah Clayton wasn't your normal, happy teenager. Her mother passed away when she was six. Her dad, John Clayton, then decided to move back to New Orleans, La. Now relocating is part of life. Everyone has one. But Sarah had a special gift. She could talk and see spirits. So moving to one of the most haunted cities in America really didn't appeal to her.

But Sarah's ghosts weren't your angry, throwing-dishes type of ghost you see in the movies. These were friendly, helpful, and often annoying. These gentle souls chose to stay and help the ones who are truly lost and confused. They helped these lost souls find the angel that would walk with them as they made their way from one life to the next. The Grim Reaper. And yes, he is an angel. But let's face it, you really want to make that trip alone?

John didn't want to live in the city. Instead, he found a beautiful Victorian home at the outskirts of the busy city. This was a very old neighborhood. Most of the buildings have been abandoned. Some had already been destroyed by weather, or overgrown trees. And people who just like tearing walls down. Most of the residents had lived in their homes all their lives. Once it was the center of the city, but the need for more high-rise buildings had slowly shifted the city to the southwest. Grocery stores, schools, banks, and the post office remained, and really, these made life easier. The large amount of abandoned houses, old businesses, and the amusement park supplied all the fun a teenager could handle…

And, of course, being New Orleans, everything was haunted.

Sarah's life slowly settled into a quiet routine. John would drive to work, and Sarah would meet up with her new friends and walk to school. The storm the night before had caused her and Lori to take a different route one morning. This street caused them to pass what was left of The Starlight Theater.

"Do not go in there. It's truly haunted." Lori said as she pointed to the old building.

"Lori, every building in the place is haunted."

Sarah pointed out.

"True, but this one really is. It has a nasty history." As they walked by, Sarah thought she heard music.

"A history, what kind of history?" By this time, Sarah was all ears.

Lori took a deep breath.

"Back in 1939, the theater was filled to a dangerous level. It had been raining all day. During the main show, the roof caved in, killing one hundred and twenty people. It took the police, fire department, and two hundred volunteers almost a year to find all the bodies. But only one hundred nineteen bodies were found. The body of Maria Dalgodo was never found."

"That's terrible. Why wasn't she found?" Sarah asked.

"She was on stage, the heavy rafters fell on top of her, pushing her through the stage floor, and the rest of the roof buried her. Plus, because of the amount of rain, it flooded the entire back part of the building. The building was deemed too unstable to continue digging, so the city bulldozed tons of mud covering the area where the stage had been."

"A funeral of sorts was held. Maria's husband, William, and their three-month-old daughter, and members of her family tried to accept what had happened." Lori continued.

"And they just left her there?" Sarah asked.

"What choice did they have? They couldn't continue digging because the rest of the building would collapse."

Sarah stayed quiet. Just before the girls turned the corner, Sarah noticed a woman standing on her porch, watching them. Or more precisely, her. This story would begin five years of searching, gathering paperwork, and all kinds of problems, as Sarah was now determined to find Maria Dalgodo.

One Saturday morning, Sarah entered the New Orleans Daily Newspaper.

"Good morning," the lady behind the desk looked up and smiled.

"Good morning," Sarah replied.

"How may I help you?"

"I'm doing a research paper for my English class. Do you have anything on the Starlight Theater?"

The smile disappeared from the woman's face.

"That place is haunted." She said

"Yes, so I've been told. I'm trying to find out what really happened, and the changes in the laws that were made because of it."

The woman walked away to a large filing cabinet and leafed through it. She placed a USB drive on the desk.

"Everything was downloaded several years ago. Everything on the Starlight has been archived. Study room #4 is open. If you need to copy anything, it's five cents a page."

"Thank you." Sarah smiled.

She sat down in the soft leather chair and inserted the drive. There it was. The investors, blueprints, and contractors. Everything. Sarah read about all the acts that had passed through the theater. Seven years of history. Then the big black headlines crossed the screen.

The roof caves in at the Starlight Theater after heavy rains proved to be too heavy. Killing one hundred twenty people. Police, firefighters, and volunteers have begun the heartbreaking job of finding the bodies. The outraged families demanded to know why. Sarah read all the articles. For a solid year, volunteers shoveled mud, metal, glass, cement, fractured wooden beams, and everything else the destruction did. The red velvet seats, thick heavy drapes.

The workers finally got to the point that nothing more could be done as the building became too unstable to continue. It was reported that all the bodies had been found, except one. The body of Maria Dalgodo, who had been on stage, had not been found. The heavy timbers that had held up the ceiling had pushed her through the stage floor, and more than half of the roof had buried her. The work could not continue without causing the heavy back wall to collapse and potentially killing more people. Bulldozers pushing dirt and pounding it as flat as possible marked the end of the search. One month later, family, friends, and survivors stood in front of the mound that had been created.

The mayor and the city council had donated a headstone and placed it on the grave. The priest gave a heart-filled sermon, praying that Maria would rest in peace, adding a prayer that someday someone would find her and give her a proper funeral. Sarah read about all the people who flooded William Dalgodo's home with food, tears, and offered any help they could.

When she had finished, Sarah became more determine to find Maria.

CHAPTER 2

Every night, Sarah stood in front of the Starlight Theater trying to contact Maria. There had been no one to teach her how to block out all the other voices fighting to be heard. The sound in her mind was loud and made no sense. Everyone was talking or screaming all at the same time, and Sarah started to think she would never be able to contact Maria.

Here, in New Orleans, the sheer amount of spirits was just overwhelming for her. Then, one day, while Sarah was shopping, a woman approached her. Sarah recognized her as the woman who had watched her that day on her way to school.

"You need to learn to clear your mind first," the woman said.

Sarah looked at her with surprise.

"I'm sorry," she said.

"You need to learn to clear your mind before you can reach the spirit you're looking for," the woman repeated.

"I don't know what you're talking about." Sarah's voice shook as she tried to convince the woman that she was wrong.

"Sarah, child, I know you're secret," the woman smiled. "You see, I have the same secret."

Sarah stared at her.

"You…you can talk to them?" she asked.

Her voice was just a whisper. The woman smiled and nodded her head.

"I've never met anyone who could …you know…" Sarah looked around, scared that someone would hear them.

"I can help you," she smiled. "It's really not that hard. Summer vacation will be here soon. Come to the house. We can perhaps help each other."

The woman smiled, and Sarah felt relief at the thought that she wasn't as strange as she thought.

The first Saturday of summer was cloudy and hot. Sarah walked the three blocks to the woman's house.

"Come in, child," she said.

"Have you had anything to eat?" She motioned towards the kitchen.

"No ma'am," Sarah said. "I'm sorry, I feel silly, but you know my name, but I didn't know yours." Sarah shifted in the chair as the woman placed a cup of tea in front of her.

"Thank you."

"Kathern. Kathern Jackson," she sat down across from Sarah. "Nice to finally meet you. I've heard some things about you."

Sarah looked at her with wide eyes. She didn't know many people around here.

"I don't understand," she said. "My dad and I haven't been here very long." Kathern smiled.

"Not through the normal gossip. From different places."

Sarah looked at Kathern.

"Different places?" she asked.

"The spirits gossip too. Just as bad as the living. Only they don't lie or make up stories," she laughed.

"And just what have they said about me?" Not sure she really wanted to know.

"They came to me because they knew you needed help. That you were trying to contact Maria Dalgodo." Kathern took a sip of her tea.

Sarah turned her head and looked out a window, then back at Kathern.

"You're the first person I've met that can talk to them."

She began, "Usually, if someone contacts me, it's because they have pushed their way into my mind. I've never wanted to contact anyone special. Not even my mother."

She looked away again. Kathern watched her guess for a moment. "I'm not going to lie to you. Learning to communicate with anyone who's passed isn't going to be easy. You will experience very painful headaches for the first month. But in time, it will get easier, and the more spirits you contact, the easier it will get. Some will even help you. If you contact an individual, instead of random spirits, it gets much easier. But one thing at a time."

Sarah nodded. "Is there anything I can do about the headaches?" She asked.

"Yes, I have a strong tea you can drink about thirty minutes before we start. And then thirty minutes later. But you need to eat a healthy meal before and after. This keeps your body from completely draining all your energy. And, we can't do this every day. We will set a schedule for you. You will have to rest until you build up the strength in both mind and body. A healthy diet will be necessary. I'll make a list of the best foods for you."

Kathern and Sarah started meeting every day at first. Kathern began walking Sarah through the steps of clearing her mind and focusing on one thing. Sarah changed the way she ate, buying the foods Kathern had suggested.

After several weeks, Sarah sat in the sunlit living room of Kathern's house.

"What do you know about your family history on your dad's side?" Kathern asked.

Sarah thought about it for a long moment.

"Very little," she said, "Dad's parents passed away when I was a baby. He has a brother, older than him, in California. They haven't spoken in a very long time. Something about an argument."

"Has your dad ever said anything about his mother?"

"Not really. His parents were from here. Had a house further south. He mentioned once that his mom talked to herself."

Sarah looked at Kathern. "She could talk to ghosts!"

Kathern shook her head.

"It's a gift that's passed down to daughters. Special abilities."

"Like, what kind of abilities?" Sarah asked.

"The ability to see 24 hours into the future, or the past. Touching a person and seeing what they may be hiding or scared of."

Kathern shook her head again. "We need to sit down and talk to your dad about many things. But, today, let's try to connect with a spirit."

Sarah drank the tea, then waited half an hour. She sat back in a large overstuffed chair. Closed her eyes, cleared her mind. At first, it sounded like a large crowd of people talking all at once. Slowly, Sarah began shutting out the whispers, the murmurs, and different languages; she blocked out the ones who screamed. Then, suddenly, she heard a name.

"Ralph." She said,

"Ok, concentrate on Ralph. Call him." Kathern encouraged her.

"Ralph, hay, hello." Sarah made a motion as if she were waving to him.

Then silence.

Sarah watched as a shadow approached her. At first, it seemed like a thick fog. Then the image of a young man came into focus. He was tall, with long, straight, dark red hair. A bandanna around his head. He was wearing a T-shirt and hip-hugger bell-bottom pants.

"Who are you?" He asked. "Do I know you?"

"No, you don't know me. I heard your name, you're looking for something."

"Yes, Sally's ring. I dropped it in the car. I heard a loud horn, then nothing."

"Ask him his last name, the date. He doesn't realize he's dead." Kathern's voice sounded as if she were talking through a tunnel. "Don't tell him anything. Just that you will help him."

"Ralph, what's your last name?" She asked. "And the last date you remember. Where was the car parked when you heard the horn?"

Ralph thought for a long time.

"Cooper, I'm Ralph Cooper. It's summer, July 18, 1965." He sat down on nothing and crossed his legs. "I was on my way to Sally's house. I was going to ask her to marry me. I... I bought her a ring. I was looking at it when I hit a bump and dropped it. The car stopped, and I bent over to the passenger side to look for it. Then this loud horn, I covered my ears, then nothing. I can't find the ring or my car."

He stood up and looked around. "I have to find my car and Sally's ring."

He turned around and walked away from her. He slowly faded back into the dark and then was gone.

CHAPTER 3

The lady behind the desk smiled as she handed Sarah the newspaper articles dated 1965.

"Back again," she smiled.

Sarah smiled back and shook her head. It took several hours before she found the article she had been looking for.

Young man killed, when car stalled on a train track.

Ralph Cooper was killed Saturday night when his 1963 Chevy stalled on the train track just south of New Orleans on Highway 45. According to police, Mr. Cooper was leaning towards the passenger seat and didn't see the silver passenger train coming towards him. Mr. Cooper, 21, is survived by his parents, two younger siblings, and his longtime girlfriend, Sally Jackson.

To Sarah's surprise, there was a picture of the car. Ripped in half from the violent hit from the rain. But you could see the license plate.

LAR 269.

The paper even told where the car had been towed to. So for the next month, Kathern and Sarah walked up and down rows and rows of wrecked cars and trucks. He liked music, movies, and his job. Then it happened. The rear end of the car.

"Sally," everything you never wanted to know about a person. But the two women never said anything. They just listened to him. Then it happened, they found the rear end of the car.

'There… there it is!" Ralph shouted. "My baby," he suddenly stopped.

He just stood there. "What the hell happened to my car?"

Kathern walked up to him, "Ralph, that horn you heard, it was a train."

He looked at her in disbelief.

"Sweetheart, you were hit by a train."

"That's impossible, that would mean I'm…" his voice trailed off.

For a very long time, no one spoke. Then Kathern turned and looked at him. "Yes, dear, you died that night."

Ralph stared at her. "You mean I'm dead? But I'm standing here, talking to the both of you. I can see you, you can see me. How could I be dead?"

"Kathern and I have a special gift. We can see and talk to spirits." Sarah explained to him. "Kathern is teaching me how to block out all the voices in my mind and talk to just one spirit. I heard your name and focused just on you. You needed help to find Sally's ring."

"Yes, I dropped it when I hit a bump. The train trucks. It was dark. There were no lights, no bells, no warning that a train was coming."

Sarah and Kathern looked at each other. "That's not right. There should have been all that stuff. And the long arm that comes down to stop traffic."

Kathern just stood there for a moment. "Your parents should have sued the railroad for improper equipment."

Then Sarah turned and looked at the car.

"One thing at a time, let's see if we can find that ring."

She slowly walked around what was left of the car. There was nothing left. The weather had destroyed the seat covers. Now there were only springs.

"Ok. Ralph, you said you had dropped the little box on the passenger side, so when the train hit the back passenger door, the car should have spun around at least twice. That would have forced the box under the seat and into the backseat."

She bent down and began looking into the springs of what would have been the backseat. Then she saw it… The small box had been forced hard into the top of the seat and had gotten caught there. She crawled into the frame a little further and reached up and slid the box off the spring it had been caught on.

"There, look, I found it."

She proudly held the little box up. Most of the red velvet was gone. The question was, was the ring still in it?

They all held their breath as Sarah slowly opened the lid. The tiny diamond shined like a star as soon as the sun hit it.

"Now let's find Sally," Sarah said

"Is she dead, too?' Ralph asked.

"She was eighteen in 1965. So she would be in her late seventies now. And she may have gotten married."

Ralph turned and looked at her. "Married? Why would she do that?" he asked.

"Life goes on for the living. It just doesn't stop because someone you love dies." Kathern explained to him. "You have been dead for almost sixty years, Ralph. Life as you knew it stopped. But it didn't for Sally, your parents, or even your siblings."

"Are they all dead?" he asked.

"Well, your parents, yes, your siblings, may be still alive. It depends on a lot of things. Life is a very strange thing. As a living human, anything could have happened. Accidents, illness."

"Ok, I get the picture," Ralph said. "So, what you're telling me there's really no way of finding out?"

"No, there are many ways of finding a person. We know her maiden name, her age, so we get in touch with the department of records and see if there are any certificates registered in La."

With Ralph's help, it didn't take long to find what we were looking for. Sally had passed away four years after Ralph's accident. Suffering from pneumonia. We found her obituary, which told us where she had been buried. With Ralph standing close by, Sarah and Kathern dug a small hole next to Sally's headstone and placed the box with her ring inside, and covered it up. They said a prayer, but just before they walked away, a young woman's voice came from behind them.

"Oh, Ralph, it's beautiful."

They watched as two glowing lights disappeared into the shadows of the trees.

Back at Katherine's kitchen, Sarah drank her tea in silence.

Kathern sat across from her.

"How's the headache?" she asked.

"Almost gone, thanks to the tea."

"Good, because it's time we had that talk with your father."

CHAPTER 4

This is where the fun Begins

Early Saturday morning, Sarah and Kathern sat in Sarah's kitchen waiting for her dad, John, to come downstairs.

Sarah was visibly nervous. John had never told her much about her grandmother. Just that she was a kind, loving woman. Strangers would come to their home and talk in private with her.

"She talks to herself," he said once.

As John walked into the kitchen, he stopped and stared at them.

"Good morning, Dad." Sarah smiled.

Kathern just smiled and nodded her head.

"Get a cup of coffee, and have a seat." John moved across to the counter slowly.

"Why do I get the feeling I'm not going to like this?" he said.

He sat down and waited. Kathern cleared her throat. "John, we need to have a serious conversation about your mother."

John took a deep breath. "I knew this day would come."

The two women looked at each other.

"Dad?" Sarah looked at her father. He took a sip of his coffee.

"You've come to ask me about your grandmother." He stated. Again, the two women shared a curious look.

Sarah shifted in her chair. "Well, yes."

John ran his hands through his hair and got up. A few minutes later, he returned with two large old photo albums and set them on the table. Sarah took one Kathern, the other. As they flipped through the pictures, John watched their faces turn from curiosity to not understanding, to surprise, then disbelief. He smiled as they mumbled to each other

Sarah looked at her dad.

"I'm not sure I understand," she said.

As John pointed at each picture, he explained. "This is my mother, Ella. This woman is my grandmother, Bella De' Loung. And this young lady.." he looked at Kathern, "is Bella's little sister, Tessa De' Lounge."

"That's my grandmother." Kathern choked out.

John shook his head. Sarah looked at her, "That makes us cousins?"

"Once removed," John added.

He flipped a page and pointed to a woman Sarah recognized.

"That's Maria Dalgodo." She said.

John shook his head, never taking his eyes off his daughter. "My great-grandmother," his voice whispered. The two women stared at him as if he had just slapped them.

"You're telling me... us... that we are related to Maria Dalgodo?" Sarah moved a pointed finger between her and Kathern.

And again, John shook his head.

Kathern shifted. "But my mother never said anything about this."

John ran a hand down his face. "Because you weren't supposed to know. It was to protect the family. But when Sarah started researching Maria's death, I knew it would have to come out."

"But why?" Kathern asked.

"Because some families tend to hold a grudge. For generations," he told them.

"Ok, Dad, spill the beans," Sarah said.

John took a deep breath and began the story.

"It all started soon after Maria died. Her body was the only one the rescuers couldn't find. But Maria and William had a daughter. Emma. She was three months old when her mother died. William's sister Stella started to convince William that he wasn't capable of caring for his daughter. She convinced him to give the baby to her and her husband, Robert. 'It would only be till you got back on your feet.' Stella told him. But Stella had another reason to want the baby. You see, being a very popular entertainer, Maria had money and gold jewelry worth thousands, millions today."

"She wanted the inheritance," Sarah said.

He shook his head.

"And the jewelry." Kathern finished.

"There's a problem…"John continued. "William found out what his sister was planning. He and the baby disappeared. So did Stella's husband, Richard. Four days later, a body was pulled out of the swamp. It was badly decomposed. No ID. After no missing person was filed, John Doe was buried."

"So no one knows if it was William, Richard, or someone else," Sarah said.

John looked at his daughter.

"There may be a way to find out," he said.

"How?"

"You could talk to Mama Bella?" he said.

"I know you can speak to spirits…" he said, "all of the women in Bella's family can."

"You knew?" Sarah asked.

John shook his head.

"Mother told me when you were three. I didn't say anything till we moved back here."

"So how do I get in touch with her?"

That night, John drove his daughter out to the old abandoned amusement park.

"At the far end, there's a carousel. There's a black horse, very out of place. Stand on the inside and call to her. She's going to know who you are. She has the answer you're looking for."

Sarah sat in the car for a long time, looking out at the heavy fog. Then turned and looked at her dad.

"I'm not sure I can do this. I've only contacted one ghost."

Her dad smiled.

"Don't worry. Bella will make sure you're safe."

It took longer than expected, but she found the carousel and the black horse. Standing beside it, she took a deep breath, closed her eyes, and cleared her mind.

"Great-great-grandmother, Bella," she called. "My name is…"

"Sarah," a woman's voice came out of the dark. "I know who you are, child."

A dark figure walked out of the thick fog. Slowly coming into view. Momma Bella was a tall, chubby black woman dressed in an old black dress, a white apron, and a white rag wrapped around her head. Sarah stared at her.

"Come, child, I know why you're here. I've been waiting for you for a very long time."

They walked in silence. After a while, a large house came into view. Smoke flowed out of the chimney, lights were on, and Sarah could smell chicken frying. The house was warm and very clean. Jars lined the shelves in the kitchen. It was quiet. No, birds, no bugs, nothing.

"Sit down, child. Are you hungry?" Sarah shook her head.

"No, ma'am," she said.

Momma Bella smiled.

"I can see my daughter, Maria, in you," she said.

Momma set a cup of tea in front of her. "This will help with your headaches." Sarah smiled.

"Thank you."

Momma Bella sat across from her.

"Some of the other spirits tell me, you've been trying to contact Maria?"

"Yes, ma'am. I want to find her. Give her a proper funeral. Help her find her way home."

Momma Bella smiled. "I've been waiting for my daughter for a very long time."

Her eyes filled with tears. "And you deserve to know the truth about your family."

CHAPTER 5

Sarah listened as Momma Bella explained the worries, the night the ceiling came down. The frantic search for survivors. The finger-pointing about why it happened. Families sued the city, the contractors, and Starlight's management for forcing the stagehands to lock or block several exit doors.

"But one family suffered more than any other." Tears threatened her eyes. "They never found my baby girl."

Her voice cracked on the last word. She looked away, wiping tears from her cheeks.

"Why did they stop?" Sarah asked. Momma Bella got up and refreshed the tea cups.

"The remainder of the building threatened to collapse, killing more people. As much as I wanted to find Maria, I didn't want more death's." She paused. "The contractors reinforced several walls and the ceiling. They bulldozed the ground, put up a marker, and put up signs so that no one could disturb the ground. There was a service for her. And we had to accept it."

Sarah stared out the window. Dark figures walked by, but no one spoke to her.

"The real problems started a few days later when William's sister started hounding him about his ability to take care of the baby. Emma was only three months old."

"And it was a different world then," Sarah said.

"Yes, very, very, different." Momma Bella added. "Back then, people were convinced that a man couldn't raise a child alone."

"I'm sure it was Amy who called the authorities on William." Sarah sat back in her chair.

"Dad mentioned that Amy was planning something. Something about Emma."

Momma Bella shook her head.

"Yes, child, she had made arrangements to sell the baby."

Sarah's eyes got big with surprise and shock. "Momma has eyes and ears." Momma Bella pointed to her head. "I see and hear everything. No matter the skin color, that was my grandchild. MY GRANDCHILD!!" she raised her voice.

Sarah noticed that the shadows outside vanished and did not return. "I found out what that woman was planning. Her and that husband of hers. They were going to kill William, take my granddaughter. Lie, tell people William's daughter left New Orleans, make her look as if she saved Emma."

The house shook as Momma Bella's anger rose around them. Sarah grabbed the edge of the table as her chair began to shake from the way the house moved.

Then, all was silenced, the house went still, and Momma Bella controlled her rage. But her face still showed the fury inside.

"I made sure her plans failed. I made sure she didn't get my grandchild or her money. And I made sure her husband never returned to her."

Sarah shrank down into the chair, and a cold, hard wind blew through the house. She didn't want to know. Without going into detail, Momma Bella reassured her that William and Emmy escaped the city. Unharmed. But Sarah understood Richard paid for what he had planned.

"The year had changed by then. That was 1940. It would be ten long years before I saw my granddaughter again. I made sure William could return to his home." Momma Bella sat back down, the rage within her now quiet. "But there were conditions. Changes he had to make. New Orleans never forgets. Never let go of its anger."

She told Sarah William returned using different names for himself and Emma. Was ten by now. Understood why these changes were necessary.

"But some things you can't change, can't hide. Some things need help to understand, to control, to nurture." Momma Bella emphasized the last word.

"Emma could speak to spirits?" Sarah asked.

Momma Bella nodded.

"Yes, child. Just like her mother and grandmother. Just like the child she would have. And just like the way you and I are speaking. Emma's son would have a different gift. But it came from the same blood."

Momma Bella reached across the table and rested her hand next to Sarah's. "You have questions about the difference. I see it in you. The confusion."

She smiled. "I was taken from my home in Africa. Brought here to New Orleans. I was young, scarf. Ripped from my home and family. But in a way, blessed. The man who bought me was not like the rest. He had a kind heart. On the surface, he was a very rich and powerful plantation owner. Grew cotton and orange trees. Owned many, many slaves. But very few knew the truth. Everyone who worked for him were free men. He paid them, provided homes, good food, and most important, each man, woman, and child carried papers saying they were free people."

Sarah smiled. Knowing that man didn't believe in slavery. Momma Bella took a photo album and put it on the table. To Sarah's surprise, there were pictures that her father had shown her. Momma Bella's laughter filled the house. The shadows outside returned.

"Although we could not legally marry, he was my husband in the eyes of god. My children were born with light skin. If you didn't know, to others they were white. Maria also married a white man. William knew who she was. But real love doesn't have the burden of skin color. Love doesn't hate the way people tend to do."

"Thank God," Sarah said. "Why didn't my dad tell me sooner? Why wait?"

"Your father waited until you were older. Wanted to make sure you didn't hate others who had a different skin color."

"Dad said skin color didn't make a person who they were. It's what they believed in their hearts."

"Your father is a good man." Momma Bella said.

"What name did William use when he came back?" Sarah asked. Momma Bella turned her head.

"I don't know. William and I agreed it was for the best. I would see them a few times a month, but we never spoke. We didn't want to take a chance that someone would figure out who they were." Sarah looked at her.

"You said you knew what Richard was going to do. What went down?" Sarah wasn't sure she wanted to know.

Then, Momma Bella's voice dropped very low. "My younger daughter was taking care of Emma, her older brothers helped William pack, Robert sent a message to William saying his car had a flat, and could he come pick him up. It seemed that Robert walked away; he was not in his car. That night, William and Emma left. A body was pulled from the swamp four months later."

Momma Bella didn't say anything else. She didn't have to. Sarah understood. "I watched my granddaughter grow up from afar. I was across the street when she and her husband came out of the church. She smiled at me. Emma would send messages through spirits to keep in touch."

"Not knowing their name, finding them may be impossible." Momma Bella looked at her.

"Emma married a man named Paul Clayton. They had a son and daughter. That daughter is your grandmother. Her daughter is your mother. Your dad has the answer you're looking for." They talked about other things, then Momma Bella walked her back to the carousel.

"I'm here when you need me, child." She hugged Sarah as if she would never let go. Then, the thick fog began to cover the trees. Suddenly, Sarah's dad was helping her to bed.

The sun lit up the room. Sarah slowly opened her eyes, her head was pounding.

"Welcome back," Kathern's voice sounded like she was standing in a tunnel.

She helped Sarah sit up, fluffing the pillows at her back. "Here, drink your tea. But be careful, it's a little stronger than usual."

"Wow, I'll say…" She looked around. She was in her room, in her bed. But something felt different. She couldn't put her finger on it, but something was different. She looked at Kathern, who was staring at her.

"What's wrong? Why are you looking at me like that?"

"What do you remember about your visit with your great-great-grandmother?" she asked. Sarah thought for a moment. She realized her headache was gone.

"Everything," she said, "I remember everything."

Kathern nodded. She took a small mirror from the drawer and handed it to her. Sarah's eyes grew wide. Streaks of gray ran through her hair. There was an odd mark on her cheek.

"What the …" She dropped the mirror.

Kathern smiled.

"Do you know how long you were there?" she asked.

Sarah shook her head.

"Three days, Sarah. You were in the other realm for three days."

Sarah looked at her

"No, that's impossible."

"That's what I thought, so too, and you're the only person I've ever known to do it. Your great-great-grandmother is a very powerful spirit. She protected you, made sure you stayed safe. Did you eat or drink anything?"

"Yes, we drank tea. She said it would help with the headaches."

Kathern smiled.

"That's what kept you alive, healthy."

Sarah shivered.

"And that mark on your cheek, protests to you from others that may want to hurt you."

"But I've never had…"

"You will now. My mother once told me a story about the night William left. Robert didn't just disappear. He didn't walk away from his car. Romers said he was attacked by two men. Rob Ed, beat up pretty badly. Maybe confused, he thought he was walking back into town. But walked into the swamp instead. Or thrown. Four months later, his body was pulled out of the swamp. No one was charged, but his family always blamed William." Kathern took a deep breath. "But no one knew what happened to him or the baby."

"He came back," Sarah whispered. Now it was Kathern's turn to be surprised.

"He what?" Sarah told her everything Momma Bella had told her.

"Robert was going to kill William in order to get Emma," she said. "But Momma Bella found out and made different plans."

Kathern didn't have to ask; she knew.

"I think it's time I met Maria."

CHAPTER 6

Six months after she began, Sarah once again stood in front of The Starlight Theater. Momma Bella had been a very powerful woman. Sarah wondered if Maria was like her mother. She cleared her mind and started walking into the cold, empty building.

"Maria?" she whispered.

"Hello?" There was a slight noise to her right, Sarah followed it till she was deep inside, towards the back. The building was thick with huge trees, thick bushes, and tall grass.

Then she saw it.

A dark shadow, to her right. But whatever Sarah expected, this wasn't it. The dark figure was no bigger than a five-year-old child wearing a hooded robe that was six sizes too big. The figure was struggling to free itself from a cabinet door that had the bottom of the robe caught. Sarah quietly sat down on a tree limb and watched, trying not to laugh. The figure pulled and yanked at the bottom of the robe. Once, it stopped and just hung there for a few minutes. It swung back and forth, arms crossed. Then it raised up, grabbed at the robe, and with all its might, pulled. The cabinet door popped open, sending the dark figure flying across the room and into the thick bushes next to her.

"EEEEEEEK!!" Then thud.

It was quiet for a moment, then, fighting its way out, the figure stepped out beside her, sitting down hard on the ground, shaking its head. Sarah covered her mouth, trying not to giggle. Then it slowly turned its head and looked up at her.

"Boo!" Sarah said.

The figure sprang into the air and flew back into the cabinet it had just fought so hard to free itself from. This time, Sarah couldn't hold in the laughter. Tears rolled down her cheek as she knocked on the door.

Nothing.

She knocked again.

"Come on, I know you're in there," she said.

"You not funny," a voice shouted from inside. Trying to control herself, Sarah knocked again.

"Maria. My name is Sarah. I'd like to talk to you."

"You not scare me no more?" The voice asked. She covered her mouth, then cleared her thoughts.

"Umm, no, I won't scare you again," she said.

Slowly, the cabinet door opened, and the figure poked its head out. It stared at her, not sure what to believe. Then it flew slowly towards her, stopping in front of her.

"Do I know you? You seem familiar to me," it said.

Kathern had told her not to reveal who she was. "No, we've never met."

It wasn't a lie.

"What you want with me?" It asked.

Sarah didn't know how to answer this question.

Then it asked her. "Why you can see and hear me? No one else can. Why you can?"

Sarah took a deep breath.

"I have a special gift." She said. "I can see and talk to spirits."

"My mother had same gift. You know her?"

Sarah shook her head.

"Hmmm, that funny, you got her mark on your cheek."

It pointed to her right cheek.

"You sure you don't know my mother?" Sarah thought about it.

"Ok, yes, I've met your mother," she admitted.

"Me thought so. Why? What you want with Momma Bella?"

"I had some questions about you and your family."

"What you want with my family?"

The figure moved closer to her.

"It's a long story, Maria," she said.

"I got nothing but time. I know what I am. I hear what they call me. 'Ghost.'"

It moved away from her. Sitting down, hanging its head. It sniffled a little. Sarah sat down beside it, putting her arm around the dark robe. It was quiet for a long time. Then Sarah broke the tension.

"Maria, do you remember anything about the night the roof collapsed?"

"That was a bad night, very cold." She began, "Too many people inside. And rain, rain, rain. For three days, nothing but wind and rain. We all wanted to close the theater until it stopped. We knew it wasn't safe. But, the owner said he would fire all of us if we didn't do our jobs."

Maria stood up, holding the robe up so she could walk. "I was on stage when the timbers began to split and break under the pressure. Then everyone was screaming, I heard someone yelling, 'It's going to cave in, run!' I looked up, and the entire framing came down. Then, nothing. He came for me, but I couldn't go. I didn't understand why. Then I heard the priest saying prayers. Saying I hadn't been found. I couldn't go until someone found me. So, I Waite, here, listening to time pass."

"That's why I'm here, Maria, I'm going to try to find you. You said you were on stage. Ok. Well, it's a start. I have to go now, but I'll be back soon."

Sarah and Kathern sat in the living room. The visit with Maria's Ghost was easier than she thought it would be.

"She's nothing like her mother," Sarah said. "She knows there's some kind of connection, but can't put a finger on it. There has to be a way to find out what name William was using. If we can find that, we can find Emma."

Kathern got up and took out a notebook.

"Ok." She began. "We know that Maria's maiden name was D'Loung. When she married William, she changed it to Dalgodo.

Your grandmother, John's mother, was Clayton. We need to find out what her maiden name was."

Sarah put her hand on her forehead.

"Dad has several picture albums. Maybe one picture has a name on it. It's a long shot, but it's all we have."

The long, hard task of finding pictures that had the same people in them began. Sarah pulled out the first picture her dad had shown them. Momma Bella, her sister, Ella, and Bella's four children. Toby, the oldest, then Henery, James, and the youngest and only girl, Maria.

They found a picture of William and Maria on their wedding day. There were several pictures of Momma Bella holding baby Emma. There was a picture of Momma Bella, William, and Emma. On the back, someone had written One final picture before they disappeared out of our lives. Although there were many more pictures, William was never seen again.

Weeks later, Sarah was once again sitting on her bedroom floor. Thirty or so pictures lay in a semicircle around her. It was almost three in the morning. She was tired, and had a headache. A light breeze blew her window, scattering some of them. Sarah hurried to pick them up. That's when she saw it. At first glance, it looked just like someone had taken a picture of the garden behind an old church. But as she looked at it, Sarah noticed three people standing on the other side of the fence. The woman was wearing a long, fancy dress.

Then it hit her. Not just a dress, but a wedding dress. The picture wasn't very clear, as if taken in a hurry. Sarah grabbed her phone.

"I found it!" She screamed at the person on the other end. "I found the picture we've been looking for. It's not very clear, but I believe it's a picture of William, and Emma on her wedding day."

Sarah flipped the picture over. "Oh my god, Kathern, Mr. and Mrs. Paul Morgan and Mrs. Morgan's father, Deago Williams. Emma's Madina name was her father's first name. And my grandmother's Madina name was Morgan. John's mother then married Richard Clayton, my dad's parents."

There was silence on the other end. At first, Sarah thought the call had been dropped. Then she heard the sound of Kathern softly crying. Nothing more had to be said.

"Good night, Kathern."

Sarah hung up as tears began to flow down her own cheeks. With this, they had all the information they needed. With one drawback. It was always suspected that William killed his brother-in-law, Robert, the night he disappeared. After all that was the reason that William changed his looks and name when he returned to New Orleans.

"We know he didn't kill Richard," Sarah said. She and Kathern sat at a table in a small cafe, eating lunch. "No one was ever charged either." Kathern dabbed her lips and put her napkin down.

"So, no one saw what happened, no one knows the truth…."

"My great-grandmother knew." A young man's low voice startled them. "She even told the police that William was nowhere near Robert that night, but Robert's brother, Erick, never believed her."

The two women stared at him. "David, David Brinner."

He held out his hand. Sarah hesitated for a second, then shook his hand.

"Sarah Clayton." She began. "And this is Kathern Martin."

"Hello," Kathern said. "Please, sit down."

She pointed to an empty chair. As David sat down, the waitress came over. David ordered just coffee.

"So…David, how did your great grandmother know William didn't kill Richard?"

Sarah was straightforward with her questions.

"Because William was with her that night. Not… not like that, William and my great-grandmother, Theresa, and Maria were good friends. They often starred in plays at the Starlight Theater together." David explained. "Momma Bella asked her to keep William away from the swamp, giving him an allibe."

"But, because William left, the police couldn't question him."

"And Erick refused to believe they were friends; she would lie about where William was." Kathern finished.

David nodded.

"If the police took her statement, and Erick had no real proof," Sarah said, "Then why did the police ignore her?"

"Because Erick had money."

There was a defining silence between the three people.

Sarah looked out the window, "So no matter what the truth is, in the eyes of the law, William will always be the only suspect, and Robert's family will always blame him for what happened."

"Not all of them." Another voice came from another table.

All three slowly turned their heads at the same time. There, sitting alone, was an older woman. She was well-dressed and had long red fingernails. She turned slightly to face them.

"Family history shows that Erick hated William and blamed him for ruining his life."

"Why?" Sarah asked.

The woman took a deep breath. "Erick was in love with Maria."

The statement sent shivers down Sarah's back.

"According to the family, Erick was a snob. Always bragging about his status in town. Dropping names and trying to impress everyone, including Meria. But she didn't fall for his bullshit. Erika saw him for the stuck-up, selfish person he really was. And when Meria and William started dating, well, all hell broke loose." She smiled. "Erick began a smear campaign against William. Almost got him fired from the theater on several occasions."

"Holllyyy crap." Sarah said.

"Most of the family believed Theresa, and the ones who listened to Erick, were disowned, and when William returned...."

"Wait, what?" Kathern's voice was a little louder than she wanted it.

"Yes, they knew. William didn't fool anyone. Everyone knew who he was. Emma looked just like her mother. You can't hide beauty like that. Emma was the spitting image of Meria, especially when she got older. It was like looking at a tween."

The woman got very quiet. Sarah could see she was trying not to cry.

"If everyone knew, why keep up the act?" Sarah asked.

"William didn't want his daughter exposed to the publicity, the exposing questions about if Emmy would follow in her mother's footsteps. William didn't want that life for her."

Then she couldn't hold back the tears. "It was heartbreaking to watch William stand in front of the theater, at 2 am, silently telling Meria how beautiful her daughter was. How smart, that she was growing into someone she would have been proud of. Even Erick let go of his hatred of William, but by that time, they were both old men, and Robert's death didn't really matter. Erick knew the truth.

He even publicly said that Theresa had been telling the truth, that William was at her place the night Robert died."

"But William was buried under his fake name," Sarah said.

"That was at his request. He told me once that when someone found Meria, if it was possible, bury her next to him, and only then, they could change his name on his headstone."

"And Emma?" Kathern asked.

"Emma and her husband were buried next to William."

"That explains why my dad bought several plots around them. That's where his parents are buried."

The woman nodded. "Your father had no idea why his mother was so insistent on being buried in that exact part of the cemetery. But she knew. She had always known."

The woman then quietly paid her bill and stood up.

"Maria had a will, but no one knows where she had hidden it. William sold all the furniture and the house when he left and never went back to look for it. Whatever Meria had, whatever she left behind, he didn't want it. The only thing he wanted was her. Nothing more."

"That's why he never remarried," David spoke up. "He stayed with Theresa until he passed away, but never married again."

"Then there's no way of finding her will, even if we can prove our relationship to Meria," Sarah whispered.

The woman put her arm around Sarah's shoulder. "Just knowing who you are and who Meria was is enough. Meria was a beautiful, talented person. Never had anything bad to say about anyone. Even Erick, she never spoke a bad word about him. She had a smile for everyone. I'm sure even the devil himself loved her."

She smiled at David. "I truly hope this makes things right between our families. Erick caused a lot of heartbreak for your great-grandmother before he told the truth. There's been an uneasiness between our families. I want the ones who have passed to be able to really rest in peace, knowing we can end this. Be able to let go of the past and move forward without the anger that Erick created."

David stood up and enveloped her in a tearful hug. He looked at her with soft eyes that finally found forgiveness.

"Yes, it's over between our families. No more grudges, no more anger. We can build a new, better relationship between us and our future children." He smiled at her.

"Thank you, David, thank you. Carrying this burden was so hard for me."

"Put your burden down, carry it no more. Lift it off your family's name. Only say Erick was blinded by hatred, but made it right, and that's what counts. He told the truth, redeemed himself, that took a lot of courage to stand up and admit he was wrong. That's something to be proud of."

They hugged again, and she walked out the door, head held high, with a new vision of her future.

That night, Sarah sat and told Meria's ghost what had happened between the families. The little figure sat next to her, quiet, for a long time.

Then she floated up and nodded her head. "The spirits will rest easier from now on. No more crying, no more burden to carry. It is done for all of us."

She slowly retreated into her hiding place. Sarah could feel the difference in the air. It was lighter and happier, like the air after a storm.

That night, she went home and lay on her bed, eyes wide open, pondering her interaction with Maria's Ghost. She was reminiscing in her thought and suddenly she felt the air feel a little heavier. A dark figure appeared and looked at Sarah. She found herself in disbelief at what she was witnessing.

"Are you…" She said.

Before she could even finish, the figure said, "The Grim Reaper."

Sarah stuttered, "Holy… You're really…"

"Why are mortals scared of me? I don't understand." The figure questioned.

"I mean, you do take souls; nobody wants to die."

"You're mortals, you're here to leave one day. I am just here to walk with you through a passing. I AM NOT THE ONE TAKING THE SOULS, MORTAL!" He sounded angry.

"I am sorry for misunderstanding. It's natural for people to be scared of you."

"It's denial of the mortal to think they're eternal."

"I guess, did Meria send you?"

"Speaking of Meria…"

Before Sarah could even comprehend, she went into a state of being motionless. Then a large room appeared with several people sitting and talking. There was a baby. Then the picture changed. Another room, a study room perhaps. A shadow appeared. It slowly came into focus, Meria. She turned as if she knew someone was watching her. She pointed to one corner of the room.

There, an old roll top desk stood. Meria walked over and bent down, pulled out the bottom drawer, and emptied it. Taking a thin butter knife, she revealed the drawer had a false bottom. Meria then held up a large envelope and placed it inside, replacing the bottom. Meria then stood up and nodded. The vision went dark. Sarah looked at the reaper.

"The will, it's in the bottom drawer of that desk." The reaper shook his head.

"How can I find it, I mean, may not even exist anymore."

The reaper started moving back into the shadows, "It's close, Sarah, you have seen it. You just have to open your eyes."

Then he was gone.

Sarah was left speechless.

CHAPTER 7

The sudden stream of sunlight woke her up. She sat up and looked around her room. She didn't remember lying back down or falling asleep. Just then, the doorbell rang. Sarah looked at her clock. 6:30, who would be here at this early hour?

"Kathern," her father's voice floated up to her room.

"I'm sorry to bother you so early, John, but I need to know if Sarah's alright."

Then Sarah's voice came from the top of the stairs. "I'm fine, Kathern."

Kathern looked as if she was going to cry. Sarah was still slipping on her robe when Kathern engulfed her in a bear hug. Sarah returned the hug.

"Kathern, what is it? What's wrong?"

"I'm fine," she reassured her friend.

John took Kathern by the hand and helped her into the kitchen. Filling the copper kettle, he put it on the stove, then retrieved three cups and placed them on the table. Kathern's hands were shaking. He reached across and placed his hands on top of hers.

"Kathern, tell us what has gotten you so shook up?" his voice was calm and gentle.

She looked up at him, then at Sarah. "I felt him, he was here. In this house."

John looked at her.

"Who was here?" he asked.

Sarah's voice was low.

"The Grim Reaper," she said. "He came into my room last night."

John didn't mean to shout, "He what?"

He stood up so fast his chair fell backwards, hitting the floor with a loud thud. Sarah saw the fear in her father's eyes.

"Dad, it's ok, he didn't come for that. He came to help. He showed me where Meria had hidden her will."

Her father looked at her as if she had just run over his dog.

"He came to help? You've gotta be kidding me? Tell me you're kidding me."

Sarah looked at him and smiled.

"No, I'm not kidding," she said.

The whistling of the kettle brought him back to reality. His hands were shaking as he poured hot water into each cup, still in shock from what his daughter had just told him.

"I've never heard of him being helpful before," he admitted. His tone was flat.

Sarah smiled as she sipped her tea.

"Dad, that's the whole idea behind what he does." She began. "He's not evil, his job is to be nothing but helpful. He's the spirit that walks with you, keeps you company, tells you everything will be alright, that there's nothing to fear. Think about it, who really wants to walk that path alone."

Her father looked at her for a very long time, and Sarah could tell he was trying to wrap his head around what she had just told him. He had never really looked at the reaper in that way. But now, it made more sense than the stories he had grown up with.

"You know, it hurts his feelings when someone calls him the angel of death," Sarah said.

"It hurts his feelings?" John repeated. "You're kidding!"

He began to laugh. "You're not kidding, are you?"

Sarah shook her head. "No, I'm not kidding."

Sarah tried to keep the anger out of her voice. "He's not evil, that's something humans made up because of their own fear of dying. They don't know the truth, the reason God made him."

That morning, a new understanding of the Grim Reaper had formed.

It was almost graduation day. Sarah was busy getting ready. Her dad had bought her cap and gown. The first time she tried it on, he cried.

"Your mother would have been so proud of you," he said.

Sarah smiled. "She is." At first, he looked puzzled.

"I've spoken with her on several occasions. She's very proud of you, too. She knows it hasn't been easy to raise someone like me."

He looked at her.

"Someone like you?" he questioned. "You mean hard-headed, stubborn, strange school friends, and even stranger boyfriends…." he began to laugh.

Sarah blushed.

"You know what I mean." he took her hand, kissed her forehead.

"I know what you meant, Sara, but remember my mother talked to ghosts, your mother talked to ghosts. It's not strange to me. Now, if you didn't have your mother's gift, then it would have been strange."

Her eyes filled with tears. "I love you, Dad. And mom wants you to stop wearing the ugly green shirt."

"Of course she does. She always hated that shirt."

They both began to laugh.

Several blocks away, Kathern had begun going to every single antique store in New Orleans, looking for a 1937 roll top desk with a false bottom. Although she had found three from the same time, none of them had the false bottom she was looking for.

"I didn't realize how many antique stores were in this city. And now I know the difference between "antique" and "secondhand. Which is about two hundred dollars."

She sipped her tea slowly.

"I'm sorry, I know I haven't been much help." She said, "Sarah, dear, I'm not complaining. I know you have been busy getting ready for graduation. This is one of the proudest days in your dad's life, and one of the saddest. His little girl is all grown up. Ready to take life by the horns. Move out, get her own place, start her own life."

Sarah looked at her.

"Whoa, hold on a minute. You're getting way ahead of yourself and me. I haven't thought of any of those things. Well, except the job thing. But moving out? Leaving dad alone in that big house?"

"Maybe you should. Sarah, don't you think it's past time your father had a life of his own? Get back into the land of the living."

Sarah looked at her.

"Sarah, your dad has done a fantastic job raising you. But he's done it alone. Your mother is upset that John hasn't…. You know…." she trailed off.

"Mom gave a kind of hint about it. At the time I didn't understand. But now I see what she was getting at. I just thought dad didn't want…"

"At first, he didn't want to. The thought of getting remarried bothered him. Then he wasn't sure how you would react to having a stepmother. Some teenagers feel like their dads or moms are trying to replace the missing parent. But that's not always the case. Then there's the problem of trying to explain that your teenage daughter talks to ghosts. Not sure how many women would understand that. It's not something that you hear every day."

"I can just hear dad trying to explain that one. 'Oh, my daughter is your normal teenager. Strange music, weird clothes, and, oh, by the way, she can talk to ghosts.'"

The two women started laughing. Then Kathern stood up.

"By the way, I have something for you." She started walking down the hall towards her bedroom, Sarah behind her. Then she noticed something. Just behind the kitchen door was a room she had never noticed before. The door was open. Sarah stood there, eyes wide.

"Kathern." She said slowly.

Kathern stopped and turned around.

"What is it, dear?" She asked.

Sarah pointed at the room. "Where did this room come from? I've been in this house hundreds of times and have never seen it."

Kathern walked up beside her.

"Oh, that's just a small spare room. My nephew was here for a few days, and I fixed it up for him."

Sarah turned her head and looked at her. Without looking back into the room, she pointed her finger.

"Look, do you see what I see?"

With a puzzled look, Kathern looked into the room. Her eyes grew wide as she saw what Sarah was looking at. There, standing against the wall, was a 1937-style roll top desk.

"Oh my God," she whispered.

"I don't believe it. You don't think… no, it's impossible. I bought that desk years ago at a yard sale." The two women hurried into the room.

Sarah sat down on the floor. She looked for just a second, then pulled the bottom drawer open. It was empty. Reaching into her pocket, she pulled out her phone and turned the flashlight on. She held the light close to the bottom, then she saw it, a small notch in one corner. Without looking up, she asked Kathern to bring her something long and thin. Kathern rushed into the kitchen and returned with a long flathead screwdriver. It took Sarah several tries, but she finally popped the bottom of the drawer up. They just stared.

"Oh my god!" Kathern whispered.

Sarah reached in and pulled the envelope out. Looking up at Kathern, "This is the envelope I saw. The one Meria had hidden."

They stood in the room and cried.

CHAPTER 8

It all came down to this. All the endless searching, funding the lies, the truth, the strange looks people would give them when going in for the DNA tests. Tests that proved beyond a shadow of a doubt that Sarah and her father were blood related to Meria and William Delgado, and Kathern was related to them through Meria's sister. No one looked at them with doubt now, only respect.

It took a few weeks to find the correct attorney. The one who had continued the law firm that his great-grandfather had started. The one who had drawn up the will. His office was in one of the oldest buildings in New Orleans. Attorney Stephen Reynolds stared at the papers he held. Adjusting his glasses. A solemn look on his face. Then, with a deep breath, he picked up the phone and called his secretary.

"Jenny, I need you to do something for me, and you're not going to like it. I need you to go to the law library and find the file for what Meria Dalgodo filed back in 1036 with this law firm."

There was a long silence on the other end.

"I'm sorry, what did you just say?" The woman's voice was filled with disbelief. "Please tell me you just didn't ask me to go to that place."

Mr. Rentolds took off his glasses and rubbed the bridge of his nose. "Jenny, I promise I'll make it up to you. Nice big bonus."

"Nothing, then, I hate you."

Click.

He looked at the three people who obviously didn't understand.

"The law library is where all the old cases, unsolved murders, and missing persons are kept. They were carefully transferred onto a USB, and filed by case numbers, or attorney's name, or law office.

However, the building is very, very old. There's black mold, dust thicker than mud, there's a time limit for anyone looking for a certain file. Hazmat suits may be involved."

John looked at him. "Hazmat suits?"

He repeated. "Your bonus should be better than big."

Mr. Reynolds shook his head. He began to explain other things, but something caught Sarah's attention. She stood up and stepped over to the wall that was filled with pictures of Mr. Reynold's family, the building when it was newly built. Pictures of New Orleans back in the thirties. Then one picture caught her eye.

"What's this picture of Mr. Reynolds?" She pointed at the black and white picture. The attorney stood up and walked over to see what she was looking at.

"Oh, that's the inside of the Starlight Theater on opening night. The pride and joy of New Orleans."

Sarah stared at it.

"It's beautiful," she said as he sat back down and began to explain the process when the proper files were found.

Sarah watched as the picture of the Starlight Theater began to move. She watched as the roof caved in and hundreds of gallons of water that had accumulated from days of rain flooded the dining room. People panic, running in every direction, pushing anyone who stood in their way. Their faces as they realized many of the exit doors had been locked or blocked off.

Then Sarah saw Meria. She had been on stage that night. She watched as the huge iron beams that the spotlights were attached to broke off and dropped on top of her, forcing her through the floor and into the spaces under the stage that were used as storage. The picture showed the passing years. Rain floods, hurricanes. It showed how the land where the stage had once been shifted, changes with each passing year and the harsh weather that came with it. Then it stopped. Clear as day, the picture stopped moving. Now it showed what the land looked like the first time Sarah saw it. The trees, bushes, and flowers, she recognized the place where she first watched Meria fight to free herself from the cabinet where she always hid.

"Oh, my God!" she screamed.

John and Kathern jumped up and hurried to her side.

"That's why she always goes back into that cabinet. She's there. When she fell through the floor. She got trapped in the storage space under the stage. The answer was there all these years, and no one realized it."

She turned and looked at the three people staring at her. "Dad, I know where she is. We can finally end this, lay her to rest beside William and Emma."

Mr. Reynolds was on the phone demanding the proper equipment, permits, and permission to do whatever it took to find Meria Dalgodo's remains.

CHAPTER 9

Convincing everyone wasn't easy. Sarah found herself explaining to the city council how she knew where Meria was. The fact that she had spoken to her many times.

"Young lady, you honestly want this council to believe that you can talk to ghosts?"

The mayor gave her a hard, cold look. Then, from the back of the room, a voice cut through all the chatter.

"Mayor Philips, we live in New Orleans, La. The home of Merie LaVoe. And the fact that Sarah Clayton is blood-related to Momma Bella Labroun, it shouldn't be that hard to believe."

Mayor Phillips stared at her.

"Is that true, child?" Sarah shook her head.

"Yes, sir. Momma Bella is my great-great-grandmother. Meria was her daughter. The baby Meria and William had, Emma, is my grandmother. My dad's mother."

Sarah turned and pointed at her father. "Kathern Steveson is the great-great-granddaughter of Meria's sister." The entire room erupted, the media went wild, and each reporter fought to get a perfect picture of the family.

At this discovery, the mayor had no choice but to give them permission to let them dig in the spot where Sarah said they would find Meria's remains.

CHAPTER 10

The air was filled with excitement. People from all over New Orleans had heard the news about the girl who had finally figured out where Meria Dalgodo's remains were.

In the weeks that had passed since Sarah had watched the picture move, her attorney had pressed the mayor of New Orleans to lift the no-digging law and allow building inspectors to walk around the building and see if they could, indeed, find Meria's remains without causing the walls to completely fall and lose this chance.

Seven of the state's top inspectors were brought in to inspect every inch of the building. Because of the massive amount of trees, bushes, and other vine-like plants, everyone was surprised by how much of the Starlight Theater still stood. Along the northwest corner, however, the structure had been broken open during the original excavation. Bulldozers had pushed through that section, leaving behind a rough, uneven gap packed with hardened mud and debris. It was through this opening that Sarah now found her way inside, stepping carefully over the broken ground as the silence of the abandoned theater closed in around her.

"Between this section and halfway to the back wall," Sarah explained to the supervisor. Taking the yellow caution tape, Sarah taped off the section of land where the cabinet was.

"Just this part. I don't need the entire building," she said.

The supervisor spoke to the inspectors, who then began looking closely at the red brick structure.

"The entire east wall no longer exists."

CHAPTER 11

In a rare moment of quiet, Sarah finally found a moment to talk with Meria's ghost.

"Meria?" Sarah carefully made her way through and around the machines.

"Meria?"

Slowly, the cabinet door opened. Just the very top of the dark hood appeared.

"Who is it?" The soft voice came.

"Meria, it's me, Sarah."

The little spirit slowly floated up and towards her.

"What's happening, Sarah? The air feels strange. And all the noise. I'm not understand. And I'm frightened."

Sarah sat down and smiled.

"There's nothing to be scared of, Meria. These people are going to help me find you."

The spirit tilted its head.

"Find me?" she asked.

"Yes, I know where your remains are. We are going to find you, bury you beside William and Emma."

"I be able to leave this place? Walk with the Reaper, and find my family."

Sarah's eyes filled with tears

"Yes," she whispered.

"Oh, ok."

This wasn't the reaction Sarah expected. She thought the little spirit would be happy, fly around, and shout. But it was quiet, next to her, the hood resting on its sleeves.

"Aren't you happy? You won't be alone anymore, and you'll be with William and Emma."

"I never thought anyone would find me. Thought I would always be here. Now I don't know what to expect."

"Except to finally be a happy little ghost," the deep voice came from the shadows.

Sarah could barely make out the figure in the trees. The Grim Reaper stepped out into the moonlight. "This is one walk I have waited for. A journey I will get to complete. Get you home."

Sarah looked at the spirit. "See, everyone wants you to rest like you should. Hopefully by this time tomorrow, everything will be as it should be."

CHAPTER 12

The construction crews managed to cut or try that were necessary. Creating a path for bigger machines to get through and begin moving tons of hard clay and dirt. This took several weeks. The weather in La did not want to make things too easy. But finally, it gave up, and the excavation continued. In time, it gave way to a crew with shovels who had their chance.

Sarah, Kathern, and John stood by, nerves on end as the cabinet was unearthed. Meria's Ghost floated close to Sarah. Then Kathern noticed something.

"Sarah, look!" She pointed to the dark figure who was apparently slowly fading. The dark figure looked down and watched as it became more transparent. Then Meria's ghost looked at Sarah, raised her arm, and just the tip of the robe waved, then it was gone.

The sound of metal hitting something solid brought her back.

"It's here, we've uncovered bones," one of the workers said.

With great care, Meria's remains were gently dug out and carefully placed in a large box that didn't fold when moved. It didn't take long for the coroner to identify whose bones they were.

"Without a doubt, it's Meria Dalgodo," he announced with a smile and tears.

CHAPTER 13

All the affected families of the history of Meria's story stood side by side with a newfound knowledge that everything about their past had now been brought to light. The truth was set in police writings. Everything was put right, and in the past where it belonged. Now, they stood in silence, tears came freely, as Meria's coffin was lowered down, resting next to William and her daughter.

The city replaced the headstone that now bore William Dalgodo's name. But there were more at this ceremony than most could understand. Slowly, the forms of Momma Bella, William, Emma, and John's mother appeared. Even Ralph and his girlfriend appeared. Sarah watched as Meria appeared. Not the little dark hooded spirit she had come to adore, but as her true person. The slender, dark-haired woman she had been in life. Sarah and Kathern watched as their family became whole once more. The priest finished the prayers that completed the ceremony.

"A Man," the crowd spoke in one voice.

Hugs and chatter, and laughter rang out as they made their way to Sarah's house for lunch. And talks about the future as all families do. Kathern left Sarah alone to say her goodies.

"Thank you, Sarah," Meria whispered. Her form became solid as she wrapped her arms around her.

"I'm going to miss you, Meria."

Sarah choked through tears.

"Don't miss me, I will always be close to you. I am always watching my family." Meria reassured her. All Sarah could do was shake her head and smile.

"Meria, come on, we have lots to catch up on." William's voice called to his wife.

One by one, the spirits hugged her, then walked into the trees and disappeared. Sarah stood for only a moment, then turned and joined the others as they got into cars and drove away.

An unseen shadow moved from its hiding place. It watched as everyone laughed and hugged one another.

"Finally." A second dark figure appeared, "She can rest. Yes."

"Now there is only one more mistake that needs to be resolved, and all the families will be as they should have been."

The figure turned and spoke to a third figure. "This too, will take time, but if we can help them along, it will be much easier. Ralph, your sister's son, is now the same age as Sarah; you need to make sure they meet within the next two years. Their union will create the child who will bring the family full circle."

"Yes, Momma Bell. I'll make sure it happens."

The three figures watched as all the families got into their cars and drove away.

Then, with a step back into the shadows, they were gone.

--------------------------------THE END------------------------------